Praise for the Shetland novels

'*Raven Black* breaks the conventional mould of British crime-writing, while retaining the traditional virtues of strong narrative and careful plotting'
Independent

'Ann's characterization is worthy of the best writers in the field . . . Rarely has a sense of place been so evocatively conveyed in a crime novel'
Daily Express

'A most satisfying mystery set in an isolated and intriguing location. Jimmy Perez is a fine creation, and I hope Ann Cleeves' Shetland series will be with us for a long time to come' Peter Robinson

'*Raven Black* shows what a fine writer Cleeves is . . . an accomplished and thoughtful book'
Sunday Telegraph

'A carefully constructed, atmospheric and interesting mystery' *Literary Review*

'Cunning character-play and deception play their part in this satisfying tale, bringing about a denouement that turns everything in the plot neatly and bewilderingly on its head' *Scotsman*

TOO GOOD TO BE TRUE

Ann Cleeves is the author behind ITV's *Vera* and BBC One's *Shetland*. She has written over twenty-five novels, and is the creator of detectives Vera Stanhope and Jimmy Perez – characters loved both on screen and in print. Her books have now sold over one million copies worldwide.

Before she started writing, Ann worked as a probation officer, cook at a bird observatory and an assistant lifeguard. She is a member of 'Murder Squad', working with other British northern writers to promote crime fiction. In 2006 Ann was awarded the Duncan Lawrie Dagger (CWA Gold Dagger) for Best Crime Novel, for *Raven Black*, the first book in her Shetland series. In 2012 she was inducted into the CWA Crime Thriller Awards Hall of Fame. Ann lives in North Tyneside.

www.anncleeves.com
@anncleeves
facebook.com/anncleeves

TOO GOOD TO BE TRUE

Ann Cleeves

PAN BOOKS

First published 2016 by Pan Books
an imprint of Pan Macmillan
The Smithson, 6 Briset Street, London EC1M 5NR
EU representative: Macmillan Publishers Ireland Ltd, 1st Floor,
The Liffey Trust Centre, 117-126 Sheriff Street Upper,
Dublin 1, DO1 YC43
Associated companies throughout the world
www.panmacmillan.com

ISBN 978-1-5098-0611-9

12

A CIP catalogue record for this book is available from the British Library.

Printed and bound by CPI Group (UK) Ltd, Croydon, CR0 4YY

MIX
Paper from
responsible sources
FSC® C116313

Visit **www.panmacmillan.com** to read more about all our books
and to buy them. You will also find features, author interviews and
news of any author events, and you can sign up for e-newsletters
so that you're always first to hear about our new releases.

*To the library staff who made me
an enthusiastic reader and continue
to share their passion for books*

1

The Call for Help

Jimmy Perez stood at the gate. There was a solid house at the end of the path, with a big garden and trees behind it. This would be a good place for kids to grow up, he thought. It was just getting dark and there was a light on in the kitchen. He could see the table was laid for supper with a pretty cloth and matching napkins. It all looked very perfect. His ex-wife Sarah had always liked things to be perfect. He felt a stab of envy. His ex-wife had a lovely house, money and a family. The love of his life had recently died, and the child he was raising wasn't his.

But he had travelled all the way from Shetland to the Scottish Borders because Sarah had said that she needed his help. It was too late to turn back now. Perez opened the gate and walked up the path. Sarah must have been looking out for him because the door opened before he knocked. She looked older than he'd expected. Stressed. Not so perfect after all.

'Come in. We can talk. Tom's still at work.' Tom was her husband now, a doctor.

Perez had only met him once and found him nice enough. A bit boring. Tom had a famous brother who was an MP, so perhaps the brother was the exciting one in the family. Then Perez remembered that he'd always found Sarah a bit boring too, so maybe his ex-wife and Tom were well matched.

'What is this about?' he said. 'Why all the drama?' They were standing in the hall. Close enough for him to smell Sarah's hair; the shampoo was the same she had always used.

'A woman in the village died. They're blaming Tom.'

'The police are blaming him? Or the medical authorities?'

'No!' She seemed cross that he hadn't understood. 'People in the village. There's gossip. Everywhere we go people are talking about it. Even people we thought were our friends.'

Perez wasn't sure what to say. It seemed he had been dragged away from his home just because Sarah's friends were talking behind her back. He wanted to leave this perfect house and drive straight back to Aberdeen and the ferry to the Shetland Islands. To his job as a police inspector, to his stepdaughter Cassie and their untidy house by the water.

'I don't see how I can help,' he said.

'If you can find out what really happened we might be left in peace,' Sarah said. He could see she was almost crying. 'It's not just me and Tom. It's getting to the children too. One of the kids in their school asked if their dad was a killer.'

'Are the police involved at all?' he asked.

'They were called but they decided it was suicide. Or a terrible accident. The case is closed.'

'So just give it time,' he said. 'It'll blow over. People will soon find something else to talk about.' He was already planning his trip home.

'I can't stand it. Please, Jimmy.'

A door swung open and he saw that two children had cleared a space at the kitchen table. There was a girl who looked like Sarah and had her head stuck in a book. A boy was playing with a huge box of Lego.

'Two days,' he said. 'I can't give you more time than that.' He paused. 'Tell me about the woman who died.' Jimmy Perez could never turn down a plea for help. It was almost an illness with him.

3

Sarah led him through to a living room at the back of the house, where two sofas sat close to the fire. Again, everything was tasteful and tidy. She drew the curtains. 'The dead woman was called Anna Blackwell and she was a teacher at the village school. In her twenties. A single mum. In a place like this, *that* caused gossip enough.'

'How did she die?'

'An overdose. Antidepressants.'

'And Tom was her doctor? He prescribed the medicine?'

Sarah nodded.

'It's a long jump from that to saying he was a killer. Was anything else going on?'

The room was quiet. Outside in the dark an owl hooted in the trees behind the house.

'They're saying he was having an affair with her.' She spoke quickly, as if she couldn't bear to have the words in her mouth. As if she wanted to spit them out.

'And what does Tom say?'

'I don't know,' Sarah said. 'He won't talk about it.'

'But you have asked him?'

'How can I?' Her voice was shrill. 'It would be like accusing him of murder.'

There was another moment of silence. 'Does Tom know that you've asked me to help?'

4

'No! He's a proud man. He'd hate to think I'd asked you to sort it out. He'd see it as meddling.'

'*I* see it as meddling,' Perez said. 'And I'm not sure that I *can* sort it out.'

But Sarah seemed not to hear. 'Anna lived in one of the ex-council houses at the edge of the village. I expect her neighbours will tell you all about her. Perhaps there was another man. Or you can find out why she might have wanted to kill herself. Even if nobody else is charged with her murder, that might be enough to stop people thinking it was Tom. He won't talk about it but it's making him ill. He doesn't sleep. And he's grown so thin.'

There was another minute of silence, then Perez stood up. 'I'd better make a start then.'

'Yes, yes. You should go before Tom comes home.' It was almost as if she was scared of her husband.

She opened the door to let Jimmy out. He stood for a moment on the path, looking in at the kitchen and the well-behaved children at the table. Sarah was stirring something in a pan on the stove. It all looked too good to be true.

2

The Landlady

Inspector Jimmy Perez booked into the Stone-bridge Hotel on the main street of the village. It had a public bar and a dining room already serving high tea. In the lobby he could smell chips and smoked haddock. He'd thought that his ex-wife might have asked him to stay in her home. He hadn't realised that his work was to be kept secret from her husband.

In his room he phoned Robert Anderson, a local cop. They'd worked together in Aberdeen before Jimmy had gone home to Shetland.

'What brings you all the way down here, Jimmy?'

'Well, we're all Police Scotland now.'

Robert gave a little laugh. 'So we are, but I wouldn't come meddling in Shetland.'

'The Anna Blackwell case?' Jimmy said. 'What did you make of it?'

'Why do you want to know?'

'Sarah King is my ex-wife. She's finding it tough. Apparently her family is being targeted by gossips.'

There was a pause. 'Ah well,' Robert said at last, 'I'm guessing Anna's little girl is finding it tough too. It seems there are no relatives to take her so she's gone into care.'

Jimmy thought about this. Anna had been a teacher. She must have loved kids. Would she kill herself knowing there was nobody to look after her daughter? 'Have you dropped the case?' he asked.

'Aye, there's no sign of murder. No break-in at the house. And it wouldn't be easy to force-feed a healthy woman a load of pills. Anna's daughter was at a sleepover at a friend's house, so there's no witness to what happened. It seems that Anna had drunk the best part of a bottle of wine. She didn't leave a suicide note but suicide's the way the lawyer in charge of the case, the Fiscal, is thinking. We think there'll be an open verdict to allow that it might have been an accident. It'll be kinder for the kid when she's older.'

'Do you think Anna was having an affair with the doctor, Tom King?'

'Is that what the gossips in Stonebridge are saying?' Robert sounded surprised.

'According to Sarah.'

'I'd heard that Sarah and Anna had fallen out about something that happened at the school, but there was no mention of the husband.' Robert made the row sound petty, as if the women were kids who'd fallen out in the playground.

'So you don't mind me poking around?' Jimmy asked. 'I've said I'll stay for two days. I can't give it longer than that.'

There was a long pause at the end of the phone. 'You'll do what you want anyway, won't you, Jimmy? You've always been a stubborn bastard. Just let me know if you find anything.'

The next day Jimmy Perez woke early. The first snow of winter had fallen. A light coating of white that made the village, with its backdrop of trees, look like a Christmas card.

Breakfast was fried and tasty. He thought of Cassie, who was only six but had strong views on healthy eating. Cassie was his stepdaughter and the love of his life now that her mother was dead.

The landlady, who told him her name was Elspeth, was nosy. His food came with a string of questions. She was like a hound sniffing for information.

'Are you here for the fishing?' she asked. Then, without waiting for a reply, she went on. 'Of course it's not really the weather for fishing. So maybe you're a walker? We get folk staying who have walked Hadrian's Wall and then come north of the border to see what we have to offer.'

'I used to know Anna Blackwell,' Jimmy said. He still hated lying after years as a cop, but it stopped the woman asking her questions. 'The woman who died. I wanted to see where she lived.'

'Poor lassie. What a tragedy!' Elspeth sat at the empty seat at his table and poured herself a cup of tea from his pot. Then she went on to tell him everything she knew about the dead teacher.

'She looked so young when she turned up in Stonebridge,' Elspeth said. 'Hardly more than a child herself. Not old enough to have a child of her own. Of course there was talk. But Maggie the head teacher said she was good at her job, and Freda, who used to teach the little ones, had got so fat that she could hardly get out of her chair. So it was time for someone new!'

Elspeth paused for breath. 'Some parents didn't take to Anna. They thought she let the children get away with murder. But the kids in the first class were only wee and they shouldn't be told to shut up all day. My granddaughter loved her to bits.'

'Oh?'

That was all it took to set Elspeth off again. 'Mrs High-and-Mighty Sarah King tried to get Anna sacked. Just because she's the doctor's wife she thinks she runs this place. She went to Maggie with a list of parents' names and told her they all thought Anna wasn't a fit person to look after the kids.' The woman looked sad. 'It was horrid. A kind of witch-hunt. No wonder the poor lassie got ill with stress. She came to this village full of joy and ended up like a hermit locked in her house all day. They had to get in a supply teacher to take her class for a while. Then Freda took the job on again and she's back there now.'

Jimmy Perez could see why Sarah hadn't told him about her campaign to get Anna sacked. It had been a nasty thing to do and Sarah must be feeling guilty. No wonder she was coming under fire from the gossips in the village. But he could understand too why everyone assumed Anna had committed suicide.

'How old was Anna's little girl?' He took a last bite of toast.

'Four. Anna must still have been a teenager

11

when she fell pregnant. The lassie's name is Lucy. She was in Anna's class at the school. So she's lost her mother and her teacher all at once.'

'What's happened to her now?' Jimmy already knew the answer but he wanted to hear it from Elspeth.

'They've taken her into care. They couldn't trace her family, you see.' Elspeth looked up at Perez. 'If you were Anna's friend you might know someone who could love her? Who could take her in?'

Jimmy shook his head sadly. 'I'm sorry. I didn't know her that well.'

3

The Neighbour

Outside there was a nip of frost in the air. The school was in the middle of the village just off the main street. Jimmy could hear the children's voices as soon as he left the hotel, and he saw the children when he crossed the road. They were wrapped in coats and scarves and had made a slide in the ice. Perez thought he could see Sarah's son playing with the other boys.

An older woman waddled into the yard and rang a hand bell to mark the start of the school day. Perez thought this might be Freda, the woman who'd lost her job to Anna Blackwell and was now back. For a while, at least. He would talk to the head teacher later, when school was over. It would be good to hear what she'd made of Anna.

He walked round the village making a map of the place in his head. He found the doctors' surgery in a modern building close to the school.

Three names were on the door. Thomas King's was one of them.

The small estate where Anna had lived was right at the edge of the village, not far from Tom and Sarah's house. Ten semi-detached homes formed a horseshoe round a patch of frosty grass. There were some swings and a slide. Anna had lived in number four. It had a neat garden, but Perez couldn't see inside because the curtains were closed. He was standing there, wondering if there was a way to get inside, when an elderly man appeared at the front door of the next house.

'Can I help you?' He was small and wiry, with teeth that were too big for his mouth.

'I just came to see where Anna lived,' Jimmy said.

'Did you know her?'

'Not exactly. I've been asked to find out why she died.'

'Are you a cop?'

'Yes,' Jimmy said. Because after all, that was the truth.

'Poor young thing. The women in this village are all bitches. They go to church on a Sunday, but that didn't stop them making the lass's life a misery with their gossip and their lies.'

14

'You don't happen to have a key?' Perez nodded towards the small, tidy house.

'Aye. I was the one who found her body.'

'Maybe you could tell me how that happened,' Perez said.

'I told the other police.' For the first time the old man seemed suspicious about Jimmy's role in the case.

'I know. I'm just checking that nothing's been missed.'

They sat in the neighbour's tiny living room in front of an open fire. The man offered tea but Perez shook his head.

'Did she own the house?' Perez asked.

The man shook his head. 'She rented it. One of the doctors bought it when it came on the market a few years ago. A kind of investment, I guess. A young couple had it for a few years and then Anna moved in with her kid.'

'What was the name of the doctor?' Perez asked, but he thought he already knew.

'Tom King.' Another thing Sarah had failed to tell him: that her husband had been Anna Blackwell's landlord.

'I've lived here for years,' the man said. 'I love the place. But the way they treated Anna made me feel sick. I'm not sure I can stay.'

'How did you find her body?'

'Anna's daughter Lucy had been at a friend's for the night, at a farm just up the hill. When the friend's mother, Gail Kerr, dropped her home they couldn't get Anna to open the door. I told them to wait here and I let myself in. Anna had given me a key when she first moved in. For emergencies, she said. Well, that was an emergency.' He stared into the fire.

'Where was Anna?'

'Where the police found her, of course. I called them from the house. There should be a record of that.' He looked at Perez. 'You *are* a cop?'

'Yes.' Perez took out his ID card and the man nodded.

'She was sitting in the living room,' he said. 'Slumped over the table next to an empty wine bottle and a glass.'

'Just one glass?'

'Aye.'

'What about the pills? Was there a medicine bottle?'

'Not that I saw. But I just wanted to call 999 and see if we could save her.'

'Of course.' Perez got to his feet. 'Can you let me have that key?'

The man remained where he was for a moment.

'I had to come back here and make up a story for the lassie, Anna's little girl. I told her that her mother was ill. I didn't have the heart to say that she was already dead.'

Then he went to get the key.

4

The House

Anna's house was sad. Perez could see the story of her growing depression in it. She must have painted the kitchen when she first arrived, he thought – it was bright yellow. Tom might be the landlord, but he was boring and he wouldn't have chosen anything so colourful.

As Jimmy walked around, he noticed the floors were sticky and there was dust on the book-shelves. It looked as if Anna had given up on the place. Only a bunch of flowers on the living-room windowsill showed any sign of hope. They were drooping and brown, but they would have been alive on the night that she'd died.

Nobody had been in to clean up since her death. The wine bottle had gone and the glass was on the kitchen counter. The police must have put it with the other mucky pots that stood there waiting to be washed up. Perez could imagine the woman sitting here, alone. He could believe that she'd killed herself. He decided he'd tell Sarah to take no notice of the gossips. This was not a murder after all.

In the living room there was a file on the table where Anna had been sitting when she died. Perez pulled on gloves and looked inside. There were lesson plans and notes about each of the children in her class written in neat, round handwriting. Even if she'd been ill, Anna had cared a lot about her job.

He walked upstairs. The child's bedroom had been emptied of most of her clothes. A doll lay on the bed. Perez hoped that a loved soft toy had been taken into care with her.

He looked into Anna's room, then went inside and opened the curtains and the window to let in some clean, cold air. The room was untidy. There was a pile of clothes on a chair and make-up on the pine dressing table. Along with the lipstick and perfume, Perez spotted an empty plastic bottle which had once contained Anna's pills.

He tried to picture what might have happened on the night of her death. She'd been drinking. Had she roused herself to walk upstairs? Had it been a sudden impulse to take the pills in the bedroom? Why would she then go back to her chair downstairs? It seemed a little odd.

If Anna had planned to die, wouldn't she lie on the bed? A final sleep. When Fran, the love of his life, had died he'd thought of killing himself, and had imagined how good it would be to go to sleep and never wake up. But he'd had their daughter Cassie to look after.

And Anna had had Lucy, he thought, so perhaps it wasn't suicide after all. He kept changing his mind about what might have happened here. By the bed there was a photo of a woman and a girl. Anna and Lucy. They both had dark curly hair and dark eyes. Both of them were laughing.

Perez looked at the dressing table again. Along with the clutter of make-up there was a scrap of paper. He'd missed it before because his attention had been caught by the pill bottle. The police must have been so certain Anna had killed herself that they hadn't done a proper search of the house. Or perhaps the paper had meant nothing to them.

It was a note written in pencil. It looked as if it had been written in a hurry.

Got your message. Friday 10th will be fine. Wine will be in the fridge! See you then. A x

It was in the same handwriting as he'd seen in the file downstairs. The 10th was the day before Anna's body had been found. The day she was supposed to have killed herself. Perez read the note again. These didn't sound like the words of a depressed woman. They were almost hopeful, looking forward. Like the flowers in the pretty vase in the living room.

But if Anna had written the note to confirm a meeting, what was it still doing in her bedroom? Had she never sent it? And if someone had been in this house drinking wine with Anna on that evening, why had they never come forward to the police?

He went back to the kitchen and looked in the cupboards. Anna had only brought the basics with her. This could be a student house. There were a few mismatched bowls and plates, some cutlery in a tray. Most of her stuff was still dirty on the counter. Perez was tempted to wash it up. In the cupboard there was one clean glass. It still had a white thread of cotton inside from the tea towel, so it had been dried quite recently.

He stood looking at it and pictured again the evening of Anna's death. Perhaps there had been a visitor, someone who'd had a glass of wine with Anna? Someone who had taken the trouble to wash up the glass and put it away before leaving the house. And that definitely suggested not suicide – but murder.

5

The Village

Anna's elderly neighbour must have been looking out for Jimmy Perez leaving her house, because he came to his door and shouted across.

'Everything all right?'

Perhaps everyone in this village was nosy.

'Yes,' Jimmy said. 'I'm surprised the landlord's not been in to clear the place for the next tenant.'

'Maybe the doctor and his wife thought it wouldn't look good if they were too hasty. Perhaps they're showing the lass a bit of respect at last, even if it's too late.'

'Maybe.' Perez paused. 'The local police must have asked if you were at home the evening that Anna died?'

'I'm always at home,' the man said. 'Once it gets dark, at least.'

'You didn't happen to notice if Anna had a visitor?' Perez leaned on the little wall that separated the man's garden from the pavement.

'The police asked me that too.'

'And what did you tell them?' Perez tried to keep his patience.

'That I didn't see anyone.'

Perez sensed that the man had more to say. 'But perhaps you heard a car?'

'Not a car. I didn't tell the other policemen because I wasn't sure and they were in such a rush, but I thought I heard voices through the joining wall. It could have been the television, though Anna didn't watch much TV. Music was more her thing.'

'The voices must have been loud for you to have heard them through the wall,' Perez said.

'Nah, these houses were put up in a rush just after the war. No sound-proofing at all.'

'So you could hear what was said?' Perez found that he was holding his breath, waiting for an answer.

'Nah, nothing like that. Just a murmur of voices. Nobody was shouting, and like I said, it could just have been the telly.' The old man stamped his feet to show that he was feeling the cold and disappeared inside.

It was still only mid-morning. It must be playtime at the school, Perez thought, because he could hear the children's voices again. He didn't want to go back to the hotel and to Elspeth's questions, but he felt a need for strong coffee and a chance to think in peace.

On the main street there was a cafe. It must be warm inside because the windows were steamed up and from the pavement he couldn't see anything at all. He pushed open the door and walked into a small room almost full of women. They had taken over two of the tables and baby buggies were crammed into any spare space. Perez took the one remaining table by the window. The women seemed not to notice him and carried on with their gossip.

A young waitress came to take his order. Perez wiped a patch in the mist on the window so he could see into the street, but it soon steamed up again. He tried to order his thoughts about the Anna Blackwell case but the young mothers' voices intruded.

'I feel dreadful,' one of the women said. 'I didn't want to sign that petition to get rid of Miss Blackwell in the first place, but Sarah *is* chair of governors and she's always in the school. I thought her reasons for thinking Anna was no good must be real.'

There was a moment of silence. 'Well, we

didn't know then that Tom and Anna were such . . .' There was another pause . . . 'friends.'

'You can see why Sarah would have wanted her out of the village.'

Perez had always thought there was a lot of gossip in Shetland, but he had rarely heard anything there that was quite as toxic as this. He could understand for the first time why Sarah was so upset that she had called for his help. It must be a nightmare to face this malice wherever she went.

The talking continued. 'Do we know for certain that Tom and Anna were lovers? Gail, you knew Anna better than anyone. Lucy stayed at your house the night it all happened.'

So this was Gail Kerr, the woman from the farm who'd had Anna's daughter for the sleep-over. She was stocky, a bit older than the others, and she didn't seem to have a baby with her. She was wearing an anorak over a scruffy sweater. The others seemed to have made more of an effort with their appearances. Some were rather glamorous, shiny and made-up. They could have been in a fancy restaurant instead of a scruffy cafe.

'Well, my brother Sandy saw them walking together through the woods,' said Gail, resting her elbows on the table. 'He said they were so wrapped up in each other that a bomb could have dropped and they wouldn't have noticed.'

The waitress brought Jimmy's coffee. It was hardly warm and didn't taste of anything.

'But you don't really think he killed her?' the first woman said. 'Not Tom! He's a doctor. A kind man. He looked after my mother when she had cancer and he couldn't have been more caring.'

'It's just too much of a coincidence.' It was Gail again. 'Something weird was going on there. If the Kings didn't kill her, they drove her to suicide.'

Jimmy Perez couldn't stand any more of their unkindness. He drank his coffee in one go, paid the bill and went outside.

Next to the cafe an estate agents' office was advertising houses to let. On impulse Perez went inside. A middle-aged woman in a suit looked up from her computer screen.

He showed his ID. 'Do you manage a property owned by Doctor King?'

'The house in Woodburn Close? Yes, that's one of ours.'

'I'm making inquiries about the most recent tenant,' he said. 'Anna Blackwell.'

The estate agent turned round in her chair to

give him her full attention. 'She was the woman who died.'

'That's right,' Perez said. 'I assume she had to provide a deposit before she moved in? Someone had to vouch for her?'

'No . . .' The woman paused. 'It was a more informal arrangement.'

'In what way informal?'

'I understood that she was a friend of Doctor King's. He said there was no need for her to pay in advance. He could vouch for her.'

Perez considered this. How had Tom King met the young teacher before she moved to Stonebridge? A thought leapt into his head. Was it possible, even, that he was the father of her child?

'Do you have a previous address for Miss Blackwell?'

The woman turned back to the keyboard. 'Yes, we do have that, I think, because we had to send out a contract before she moved in.' She hit a button and a printer began to whir. She handed a sheet of paper to Perez.

The address was in Berwick, just south of the border, in England.

'I believe that was her parents' address,' the estate agent said. 'Miss Blackwell had been at university in Edinburgh and had just finished

28

her degree. She suggested the Berwick address would be the best one to use.'

Perez wondered why Anna's parents hadn't come forward to take care of their grand-daughter, Lucy, after her mother's death. He'd assumed that there was no close family. It seemed very sad that the grandparents had allowed the little girl to be sent off to be cared for by strangers. Perhaps Anna's parents were old-fashioned and didn't approve of a child born out of marriage.

Outside in the street, the village was very quiet – there were no children's voices. Soon it would be lunchtime and they would be out to play again, Perez thought. Stonebridge seemed sad without them.

6

The Farm

Jimmy Perez was thinking that he'd go back to the Stonebridge Hotel for lunch when he saw a woman leaving the cafe where he'd had coffee earlier.

The woman was alone. The other yummy mummies must still be inside talking, he thought. It was Gail, the mother from the farm, and she made her way towards a battered Land Rover parked in the wide main street. He caught up with her just before she opened the Land Rover's door.

'Could I have a word?'

She turned round and stared at him. 'Who are you?'

'I'm a detective. My name's Jimmy Perez. I'm just checking some details concerning Anna Blackwell's death.'

'But she killed herself.' Gail was still staring.

'According to the local police the case has been closed.'

Something in her eyes made him ask, 'Do you think it shouldn't have been?'

She looked at him carefully. 'Look,' she said. 'I can't stay here and chat. I've got to get home for a delivery of feed for my hens. Why don't you come too and we can talk? I might even find some soup for your lunch. I've got to come back to Stonebridge to collect my little girl from school at three o'clock and I can give you a lift back then.'

So Perez climbed in beside her and Gail drove out of the village. It seemed like a sort of escape. He realised how trapped he'd been feeling in the village with its bitchy women and the dark woods all around it.

They took a lane that rose sharply away from the river, and as they rounded a corner there was a view of a whitewashed house at the end of a rough track. 'I love this place,' Gail said. 'I was born here and I can't imagine living anywhere else.'

She parked the Land Rover in the farmyard. Perez could see sheep on the hill behind the house and hens in a small orchard beside the yard. He thought it looked like a child's idea of a farm rather than the real thing – it could have come from a picture book. Gail seemed to read his thoughts.

'It's only a smallholding really,' she said. 'My parents sold off most of the land years ago. Now my brother and I run it almost as a hobby. We're trying our best to make a go of it. Sandy has a full-time job working for the forestry commission, and that just about keeps us afloat.'

'What does your husband do?'

There was a moment's silence and then Gail answered:

'He died three months ago in a car crash. He had real plans for the place. He thought we should turn some of the buildings into holiday lets. Without him I can't seem to work up the same passion for the project, but I'll try to make a go of it as a tribute to him.'

She opened the farmhouse door and led him into a cluttered kitchen. 'Will you have some soup?'

He nodded and sat at the table. He thought how strong she must be to carry on with her everyday life when her husband had so recently passed away. Perez had been good for nothing for months after Fran had been killed. He'd just brooded.

'Lucy Blackwell stayed here the night Anna died?' he asked.

She nodded. 'My daughter Grace is best friends with Lucy. They're both only children, so it was good that they each had someone to play with. Lucy loved it here. All this space is perfect for children and she enjoyed helping with the animals.' Gail slid a pan onto the hotplate of the range. 'Grace is so sad that Lucy's moved away.'

'Were you and Anna friends?'

Gail turned away from the stove to face him. 'Well, we didn't have a lot in common. Anna was young enough to be my daughter. I was forty when I had Grace. John and I married late. And I've lived all my life here, and Anna was English and had moved around. But we got on OK. She was great with the girls and I liked her.'

'Was she the sort of woman who might have killed herself?'

There was a long pause before Gail answered. 'I wouldn't have said so when she arrived in the village last year. She was full of enthusiasm and ideas then. I was pleased that we'd have some-one young and fit to teach the little ones. Freda had been there a long time and she was still teaching in the same way as when she first started in the job. She'd taught lots of the children's parents.'

'But later?'

Gail tipped home-made soup into a bowl and set it in front of Perez. 'Later it all seemed to get too much for Anna. It can't have been easy dealing with a small child and a full-time job all on her own.'

'You seem to manage,' he said.

'Aye, well, I'm a little bit older and I have lots of friends in the village. Besides, I'm not really on my own. My brother Sandy lives here too.' Gail looked up from her soup and smiled. 'But not for much longer, it seems! He's just got engaged and he'll be moving into a home of his own.'

'You'll miss him,' Perez said.

Gail grinned again. 'I will, but he's marrying a lovely girl and they won't be living far away. Besides, Grace, my daughter, is great company now.'

There was a knock at the door. 'That'll be the feed delivery,' Gail said. 'You'll have to excuse me.'

She went out into the farmyard. Perez wandered around the kitchen. There was a picture of Gail on her wedding day standing next to a giant of a man with a beard. He must be the husband who'd died. They were surrounded in the photo by laughing friends and family.

When Gail returned to the kitchen, it seemed that she'd made up her mind to speak, because she started talking as soon as she came into the room. 'Did you know that there are lots of rumours about Tom King and Anna?'

'What sort of rumours?'

'People are saying that Tom and Anna were lovers. He owns that little house in the village where she lived, after all. And Tom's wife Sarah took against her as soon as she started at the school. It was as if she wanted to get rid of Anna as soon as she arrived.'

'Do you know who started the rumours?' Perez pushed away his soup bowl and put his elbows on the table.

'Who can tell where gossip begins in a place like Stonebridge? The stories are like weeds, they seem to grow out of nowhere and then they spread, so there's no way of stopping them.'

Gail was silent for a moment. 'When my husband died in the car crash there were rumours that he'd been drinking. It wasn't true and it's dreadfully hurtful at a time when I'm still grieving for him. I don't know who started that gossip either.'

'But you think there might have been truth in the story about Tom and Anna?' Perez remembered Gail talking in the cafe. It had seemed then that she believed the two had been lovers.

Gail shrugged. 'They've been seen together and they seemed very close. Sarah obviously couldn't stand Anna. Perhaps we've all jumped to conclusions, but it seems to make sense.' She stood up. 'I'll get you back to Stonebridge. The kids will be coming out of school soon.'

As they drove through the open countryside and into the village, Perez felt a stab of dread. It was as if he was being taken back to prison after a brief period of home leave.

7

The School

Back in Stonebridge, Jimmy Perez went to his hotel room. He wanted to talk to Robert Anderson, the local police inspector, about the cleaned wine glass in the cupboard at Anna's house. He also wanted to find out why Anna's parents weren't taking care of their granddaughter Lucy.

But Jimmy was told that Inspector Anderson was in a meeting and wouldn't be available all day. Perez left a message for Robert to call him back.

He stood at his window and watched a flurry of snow blow across from the hills. Parents had collected their children from school and were hurrying home. He saw Gail's Land Rover move away down the main street. Back outside, the light was already fading and it felt colder.

Perez left the hotel and made his way to the school. He found the main door still open. Some older children were practising Christmas carols in the school hall. A woman in reception took his name and showed him to the head teacher's office.

Maggie Redhead was in her fifties, with fine grey hair pulled into a comb at the back of her head and bright brown eyes.

'I thought this matter with Anna Blackwell was over and we'd be allowed to get back to normal,' she said. 'It was distressing enough for the kids when she died.'

Her office was cluttered, with children's books on the shelves and brightly coloured paintings covering one of the walls. Perez decided she looked like an energetic granny.

'There seems to be some question about the cause of death.' That wasn't quite a lie, Perez thought. He wondered what Robert Anderson would make of his meddling. 'I'm just taking another look at the case with a fresh pair of eyes. You know how it is.'

'Not really,' Maggie snapped. 'I don't usually lose my staff like this. They don't die suddenly, and if they do, the deaths aren't followed by gossip and bad feeling. Usually my teachers retire. The children present them with a gift on their last day and we have a party in the staff room.'

Perez smiled. 'Did you throw a party when Freda retired?'

Maggie narrowed her eyes. 'You have been poking around.'

'Is Freda glad to be back as a supply teacher?'

Maggie sat back in her chair. 'Freda has never married and the school was her life. But she's got health problems now she's getting older. She really wasn't up to coping with a class of four- and five-year-olds. The only way she could keep order was by scaring the life out of them. I was pleased when she agreed to retire. So yes, we did throw a party for her.'

'But she's back now?'

'On a very short-term basis while we appoint another reception teacher.'

'Did Freda resent Anna Blackwell?' Perez asked. 'If the school was her life, it must have been hard for her to see another, younger teacher take her place. Especially if Anna's teaching style was so different.'

Maggie gave a little laugh. 'Freda might have resented the teacher who replaced her, but if you're saying that she killed Anna to get her job back, then that's quite mad. As I explained, she'll only be here for a few weeks anyway.'

'That's not what I'm suggesting,' Perez said. 'I'm trying to find out where the rumours about Anna and Tom King started, and I'm wondering if Freda might be behind the gossip.'

Maggie took a little while to think about this. In the background, Perez could hear the children singing 'Silent Night'.

'That might be more Freda's style,' Maggie said at last. 'She was very hurt when I told her it might be time for her to consider leaving. She was going to hate anyone who took her place. And she could be bitchy if the mood took her. I can see her starting the gossip as a kind of revenge.'

Perez nodded. 'Do you know why Sarah King took against Anna Blackwell so strongly?'

'No,' Maggie said. 'That was a complete mystery. Sarah is a parent governor and she's always worked hard for the school. She helped me interview for the new teacher's post and Anna Blackwell was her choice as well as mine. We knew that Anna was new to the career, but we decided her great ideas made up for that. We thought she'd bring something fresh to the school.'

'It must have been rather a shock, then, when Mrs King turned up with a petition demanding that Anna should leave.'

'It was a nightmare! And honestly I couldn't see what the parents had to complain about. Anna was a good young teacher. But she took it to heart. All the bitching started making her ill.

In the end I could see she was stressed and suggested she went to the doctor. That was when she started taking the antidepressants.'

'Was she still working in the school when she died, or had she taken time off sick?' Perez asked.

'She'd had nearly two months off, but she was back at the time she died. She seemed better, still a bit frail but almost happy.'

Perez thought this tied in with the flowers in the living room and the hopeful tone of the note he'd found on the dressing table. He stood up to leave. 'Do you think Anna Blackwell committed suicide?'

Maggie answered straightaway. 'Not in a thousand years. She adored her daughter. There was no way she would have killed herself and left Lucy without a mother.'

'Did she ever tell you who the father was?'

Maggie shook her head. 'I never asked and she never told me. It was Anna's big secret. I've never felt the need to pry into the affairs of my staff.'

When Perez walked out into the playground, it was almost dark and the children had stopped singing. He turned to look back at the school and saw the head teacher staring out at him.

8

The Colleague

Jimmy Perez was hungry. It seemed a long time since he'd eaten the soup in Gail's farmhouse and he decided to have an early dinner. He made his way back to the hotel along the silent village streets. It was impossible to believe that anything sinister could happen in a place that was as quiet and ordinary as Stonebridge.

As he walked into the hotel, Perez saw three people – two men and a woman – sitting around a table in a corner of the lounge bar. He recognised one of the men as his ex-wife's husband, Doctor Tom King. The rest of the bar was empty, but Perez couldn't be seen where he stood in the lobby. He was hidden by a large plant in a copper pot, and he had a good view through a glass door. He stood there, feeling a bit silly. Like a kid playing hide-and-seek. He strained to make out what the people in the lounge were saying.

'This can't go on, Tom. Two patients refused to see you today, even though it meant waiting nearly a week to get an appointment with another doctor.' That was the woman. Her voice was clear, rather shrill, and easy to hear.

Perez thought she was most likely a doctor too. She had the confidence that doctors seem to carry round with them. He assumed that both the strangers were Tom King's colleagues. They must have come to the hotel to discuss the aftermath of Anna's death.

'I'm not sure what you expect me to do.' Tom King sounded drained, almost desperate. 'The police have closed the case. I've been cleared of any misconduct.'

'You must put all these rumours to rest, Tom.' It was the woman again. She sounded like a parent telling off a naughty boy. 'I don't care how you do it. Can't you get Sarah to help? I've always seen her as a pillar of the village. Surely she can persuade these gossips to stop?'

'I don't think there's anything anyone can do,' Tom said. 'We just have to hope that it all blows over and the village finds another target for its malice.'

Tom stood up, said a sharp goodbye to his colleagues and walked out of the lounge. He passed so close to Perez that the inspector was sure the doctor would see him. But Tom was so upset that he seemed not to notice that Perez was there.

Back in the lounge, the two other doctors continued talking.

'I think he's hiding something,' the woman said.

'Not murder!' The man was shocked. He was older, grey-haired. 'Not Tom! I've known him for years.'

'Perhaps not murder, but there's something he's not telling us. You'll have to sort it out, James. You're the senior partner. We can't go on like this.'

The woman got to her feet, grabbed her bag and swept past Perez into the darkness outside. The older man stayed where he was, apparently lost in thought. Perez left his hiding place and took the seat beside him. The chair was old and very comfortable. It was a chair for relaxing in.

'I was going to order some coffee,' Perez said. 'Will you join me?'

The older doctor looked surprised. 'I'm sorry, but do I know you? You don't sound as if you come from round here.'

'I'm a detective based in Shetland. I've been asked to look again at the Anna Blackwell case. I couldn't help overhearing your conversation.'

They were still the only people in the lounge, which was dimly lit and very warm.

'Ah,' the doctor said. 'We'd hoped that was all over. It seems rather a shame to rake over the case again, but I suppose you have your work to do.' He paused. 'Yes, if we have to talk, coffee would be splendid, thank you.'

Perez went to the bar to order the drinks. When he came back, balancing cups on a tray, the doctor was almost asleep. Perez set the tray on a low table and the man roused himself and held out his hand.

'James Given,' he said. 'I retire from the surgery next year. I'd rather be leaving without all this scandal.'

'Did you know the dead woman?' Perez asked.

'I only saw her once when she brought her daughter into the health centre with an ear infection.' He paused. 'She seemed a kind woman. She cared a lot for the child. That's why . . .' James Given paused mid-sentence.

Perez completed it. 'That's why it seems unlikely that Miss Blackwell committed suicide?'

James nodded.

'Gossip has it that Anna and Tom were having an affair,' Perez said.

'I don't believe that for a second!' the doctor

said. 'Really, Tom adores Sarah. They're a perfect couple.'

Perez remembered that he didn't believe in perfect any more. 'Is there anything else you can tell me?' he asked. 'Anything I should know?'

There was a moment of hesitation.

'I think Tom might have known Anna before she moved here,' the doctor said at last. 'I don't mean that they were lovers. No, there was nothing like that going on, whatever the gossips might be saying. I think perhaps Tom was a friend of her parents. It was just a sense I had when Anna brought her little girl to the surgery. She'd asked to see Tom but he wasn't free, and she explained that she'd chosen him first because he was almost like family.'

Perez thought that made sense. It might explain why Anna had moved into the rented house in Stonebridge without having to provide a deposit. He was starting to think that he should drive to Berwick the following day to talk to Anna's parents.

James Given stood up. 'The most important thing to tell you is that Tom King is a good man. All this gossip is nonsense, and I hope you can put a stop to it. If it goes on, I'm worried that we'll drive Tom away from the village, and then

Stonebridge will have lost a very fine GP.'

Perez watched Doctor Given walk out of the hotel to his car. It had started to snow again, with large soft flakes that melted as soon as they hit the ground. In the distance a dark figure stood under a street light. He seemed to be staring at the hotel as if he was making up his mind whether or not to come in. Perez didn't recognise the watcher, though something about him seemed familiar.

When the man saw Perez looking his way from the hotel doorway, he seemed to lose his nerve. He turned abruptly and hurried away.

9

The Hotel

Robert Anderson, the local detective in charge of the case, phoned back just as Perez was finishing dinner. Perez kept him on the line until he'd climbed the stairs to his room. He didn't want anyone listening in to their conversation.

'How's it going, Jimmy?'

Perez took a chair by his bedroom window. 'I had a wee look round Anna's house.'

'Did you now?' Anderson seemed annoyed by his interference. 'And what did you find?'

'I think Anna had a visitor the evening she died.'

There was a moment of silence at the end of the line. 'And what makes you think that?'

Perez explained about the note he'd found in Anna's bedroom and the freshly cleaned glass in the kitchen cupboard. 'That changes things, don't you think?'

Another silence. 'Perhaps,' Anderson said at

last. 'Are you sure the note was in Anna's handwriting?'

'Certain.' Perez remembered looking through the file in Anna's living room. 'I checked it against some lesson plans she'd written that were in the house.'

'All the same,' Anderson said, 'we'll need more than that to reopen the case. What do you plan to do tomorrow?'

'I thought I'd go to Berwick to chat to Anna's family. It seems that she knew Tom King before she moved to Stonebridge. They might be able to tell me more about the relationship.' Perez moved to the window, but there was no sign of the man who'd been standing under the street light. 'I'm wondering why they didn't offer to take on Anna's daughter.'

'They have problems of their own,' Anderson said. 'Joan Blackwell has early onset dementia, and George, Anna's father, is her full-time carer. They couldn't cope with a growing child.'

Perez thought how unfair that was. The couple had problems of their own, and now they'd lost the daughter who might have supported them. He wondered what effect their troubles might have had on Anna. Could they have caused the young teacher more stress? Might they even have driven her to suicide?

Then he thought how everyone had described Anna as a kind woman. If she knew that her parents had problems and might need her help in the future, wouldn't that have given her a reason for staying alive?

'I might go to Berwick all the same,' Perez said, 'just to find out more about her. Anna wasn't in Stonebridge for long, and I don't feel that anyone here really knew her.'

Except Tom King, he thought, and Sarah doesn't want me talking to him.

He ended his call to Anderson, and on impulse phoned his ex-wife, Sarah. She answered softly, almost in a whisper. 'Yes?'

'I need to talk to you,' he said.

'You can't come here because Tom's home.' She spoke normally now. She must have moved to a different room where she could talk in private.

'Can you come to me? I'm staying in the hotel.'

'I don't know,' she said. 'If we meet in the bar, someone might see us. This place is nothing but gossip.'

'I'm starting to realise that,' Perez said. He gave her his room number, and it occurred to him that anyone listening in would assume they were having an affair. It was easy to jump to the wrong conclusions, and perhaps that was what everyone involved in this case was doing.

Half an hour later Sarah tapped on the door and he let her in. There were melting snowflakes in her hair and she was shivering, though the hotel room was very warm. He made her tea, struggling to open the tiny plastic pot of UHT milk, and gave her his chair. The only place for him to sit was the bed, so he perched there.

'Why didn't you tell me you tried to get rid of Anna from the school, even though you were in favour of her getting the job at the start?'

Sarah blushed but she didn't speak.

'I can't help you if you don't talk to me,' Perez said.

'It was a mistake to give her the post,' Sarah said at last. 'She was too young and too inexperienced. She let the children get away with murder.' She realised what she'd said and blushed again.

'Did Tom know Anna before she moved here?' Perez felt so frustrated that he wanted to shake the truth out of Sarah. He wondered how he could have loved her so deeply, how he could have spent all those nights dreaming about her after she'd left him.

I felt sorry for her, he thought. Because she was desperate for a child and suffered one miscarriage after another. I blamed myself. It wasn't a good basis for a marriage.

Sarah looked up at Perez over her mug of tea. 'I *thought* Tom might already know her. I couldn't be certain.'

'What gave you that idea?'

'I saw them together once in the health centre just after Anna moved here,' she said. 'Tom's car was in for a service, and I'd called in to give him a lift home. Anna was in the waiting area when I got there. She didn't have an appointment – she wasn't there because she was ill. I think she was just hanging on until he'd finished work. It looked as if she was hoping to surprise him. Anna didn't know who I was – she must have thought I was just a patient – and when he appeared she called out to him: "Tom! Look who it is!" It was as if she thought he'd be pleased to see her.'

'Was he pleased?'

'Well, I was there, so he just seemed awkward. But I could tell that he knew her.' Sarah paused. 'He lied to me. He said he'd never met her and that she must have mistaken him for someone else.'

'And that was why you set up the petition to get Anna out of the school?' Perez thought how childish Sarah was. She'd been hurt, so she'd wanted to lash out. She'd wanted to make the young woman pay. Again he thought how unfair life had been to Anna.

'I looked at her daughter in that waiting room and it was like looking at one of my own children,' Sarah cried suddenly. 'Lucy had the same dark hair. The same smile. She looked so like Tom that I thought everyone in the village would see the likeness.'

'You think Tom was Lucy's father?' Now Perez understood Sarah's anger towards the young teacher. Perhaps anyone would have responded in the same way.

'I can't see that there's any other explanation,' she said.

'And what did Tom say?'

Sarah set her mug carefully on the windowsill. 'I've never talked to him about it. I was scared that he might tell me the truth.' She looked up. 'What will you do now?'

'What you asked me to do,' Perez said. 'I'll try to find out if Anna Blackwell committed suicide or if someone killed her.' He met her eyes. 'Do you think that Tom could have murdered her? Is that why you're so frightened?'

She didn't answer.

'Where was he the night Anna died?' Perez asked.

'He was out on a call. He didn't get back until late.' Her voice was quiet. 'But Tom's a doctor. He wouldn't kill anyone. And he often has emergency calls at night.' She paused again. 'I wondered if Anna was blackmailing him. I thought she might have asked him to help her keep her job at the school.'

'And threatened to make their affair public if he didn't?'

She nodded. 'In the middle of the night, when things are going round and round in my head, I start having crazy ideas like that. I think I'm going mad. That's why I called you. I have to know what's been going on, even if I find out that Tom's a killer.' She stood up. 'I must go. I told Tom I was just calling in to the village to drop a letter in the post.' She slipped out of the room.

From the window, Perez watched her run from the hotel to her car. The shadow had returned to his post under the street light, and he was watching Sarah too. Perez tried to work out where he might have seen the man before, but the memory slid away.

10

The Parents

The next morning Perez got up early and was the first person into the dining room for breakfast. The nosy landlady, Elspeth, wasn't on duty, so he was spared her questions and could eat in peace. Today he was going to visit Anna's parents at Berwick. He cleaned the ice and snow from the windscreen of his car and then headed off towards the coast. Again he felt a sense of relief and escape as he left the village. He looked out for the dark watcher from the night before but there was no sign of him.

As Perez drove east, the landscape grew greener and less snowy. The sunshine was pale and lemony and shone straight into his eyes. Anna Blackwell's parents lived in a bungalow on the outskirts of Berwick, and as he approached he caught sight of the view across the red roofs of the town and the river Tweed, then out to the sea.

Perez had phoned the night before to warn them that he'd be coming. When he rang the doorbell, Anna's father peered through faded lace curtains at the front window before letting him in.

George Blackwell was older than Jimmy had expected and quite frail. He must have been approaching fifty when Anna was born. His wife was sitting in an armchair in the overheated sitting room, staring at daytime television. On the mantelpiece there was a photo of Anna. She looked about ten and she was in shorts and a T-shirt playing on a beach, kicking a ball.

'We'll speak in the kitchen,' George said. 'Joan will be fine on her own in here. She loves that baking programme.' He bent and kissed the top of his wife's head. The woman turned briefly and smiled vaguely. 'She was a great cook before she got ill.'

The kitchen was small, old-fashioned and very clean. They sat at a table that was so tiny their knees almost touched.

'It must be very hard,' Jimmy Perez said, 'that your wife's so poorly.'

'It's only hard because she's so much younger than me, and I worry what will happen to her when I die. Anna and I talked about it. She said I wasn't to fret and she'd look after Joan when I wasn't able to.' George looked up at the detective. 'Anna must have been desperate in order to kill herself. She wasn't a girl to forget a promise.'

'I'm not entirely sure that she did kill herself,' Perez said. 'That's why I'm here.'

'An accident, you think?'

'No, I don't see how it could have been an accident.' Perez found it hard to look at the man. 'She'd had a bit to drink, but probably not so much that she'd swallow that many pills by mistake.'

'Someone killed her?' The man was so shocked that the words came out as a shout. 'Is that what you're telling me?'

'I'm saying it's a possibility. I need to ask some questions. Personal questions, if that's all right with you.'

'You can ask,' George said. 'I'm not saying I'll be able to answer. After Anna left home for university she had her own life.'

'And a child?'

George nodded. 'She was in her first year in Edinburgh. She came home one weekend and told us she was pregnant. I couldn't take it in. We'd just been told that my wife had dementia. Joan had always been so fit and she was only sixty. No age at all. We had our own problems and perhaps we couldn't give Anna the support she needed.'

'Did Anna tell you anything about Lucy's father?'

'No,' George said. 'She told us that she was going to keep the baby and raise it on her own. There was a crèche at the university. She'd manage things. I asked who the father was, but she said he wouldn't play any part in bringing up the child. It was clear she didn't want to talk about it.'

'Did you ever meet any of her friends? Women or men?'

George shook his head. 'Anna hadn't brought anyone here recently. It was difficult. Joan finds it hard to cope with anything outside her normal routine. And no one writes letters any more, do they? So we didn't get news that way. Anna would phone once a week from uni, but that was really to find out what her mother was doing. She was always chatty enough, but we never knew what was going on in her life. Not the important things.'

Perez stared out of the narrow window into a bare, winter garden, and tried to make sense of this. 'Does the name Tom King mean anything to you? He's a doctor. I understand that he might have been friendly with you and your wife.'

George looked puzzled. 'Joan's seen lots of doctors since she's been ill, but none of them are called King.'

So why, Perez thought, did Doctor James Given think that King was close to Anna's parents? None of it made sense.

George was speaking again. 'Anna was so excited to get the job in Stonebridge. She came here specially to tell us and she brought Lucy with her. She's always loved kids. We knew she'd be a teacher when she grew up. She always loved the country too – we took her out walking in the hills from when she was very young – so I thought the little village school would suit her. Recently I could tell things weren't going so well, though. She made an effort to sound bright on the phone but she wasn't herself.'

'When did you last hear from her?'

'Two days before she died.' He paused. 'I thought she sounded a bit better. She was talking about the future, about coming home to spend Christmas with her mother and me. I thought perhaps she'd turned a corner.' He smiled. 'I wondered if there was a new man in her life.'

'Did she give you a name?'

George shook his head sadly. 'She was always one for secrets, our Anna. Maybe this is one she's taken to her grave.' He turned to Perez. 'I'm glad you're looking into this, Inspector. It's good that someone cares enough to search for the truth.'

In the living room, Joan Blackwell was still watching the cooking programme. As the old man showed him out of the house, Perez thought that he hadn't gained anything new from his chat with the dead woman's father. It felt as if the drive to Berwick had been a waste of time and he was no closer to finding Anna's killer.

He was nearly at the end of the path when George Blackwell called him back. 'That new man in Anna's life . . .'

Perez stopped sharply and turned back. 'Yes?'

'I think he must have been a Stonebridge man. Local, you know. During that last phone call she said she'd decided to stick it out in the village. She'd been thinking of leaving, of finding a new job somewhere else because she wasn't happy. But she told me she didn't think she'd be moving after all because now she had something to keep her there.'

11

The Watcher

It was mid-morning in Stonebridge when Jimmy Perez got back from Berwick, and the sun was shining on the gleaming snow. He felt as if he was returning to another world, though Berwick was hardly more than an hour away. He saw this village as a place full of secrets where nothing was quite as it seemed.

On the drive back he'd been trying to piece together all he'd learned about Anna. He was convinced now that she hadn't committed suicide. She was a kind woman who cared too much about her daughter and her parents to leave them. And it seemed she'd been getting happier. She had passed the worst crisis of her depression.

But still there were too many unanswered questions for him to make up his mind what had happened to her. Who was the new man who'd become a part of her life? Perez had assumed that if she'd been having an affair with a man in Stonebridge, then the lover had been Tom King. But perhaps she'd been seeing someone quite different. Perhaps the note arranging a meeting on the night of her death had been for this other person.

Now Perez sat in his car outside the Stonebridge Hotel and considered what to do next. On impulse, he started the engine again and drove towards the farm where Gail lived. Gail was a local and a gossip, and if anyone knew who Anna had been seeing, it would be the farmer. She would have heard any rumours.

Perez found Gail mending a hen house in the orchard by the side of the yard. She looked up when she saw him. 'One of the planks is rotten. A bloody fox will get in if I don't fix it. Do you mind if we talk out here?'

'That's fine.' He leaned against one of the trees. 'It's possible that Anna was having a relationship with someone other than Tom King. Had you heard anything about that?'

She straightened her back. There was still a hammer in her hand and it made her look fierce, like a female warrior from the Norse tales he'd read as a boy. 'No! Who was she seeing?'

'I was hoping that you might be able to tell me that.'

'It must have been a married man,' Gail said. 'There'd be no need for secrecy if he was single. She'd have known that there were rumours about her and the doctor. Being seen out with a single guy would have stopped them once and for all. That would have been a good thing as far as she was concerned.'

Perez hadn't thought about it in that way, but he saw it made sense. 'Any likely candidates?' he asked.

Gail shrugged. 'She was a bonny lass. It could have been anyone. It doesn't take much to lead a man astray.'

Perez looked at her. She sounded bitter. He remembered that she'd only lost her husband a short time ago in a car crash. Perhaps he'd been the sort to find comfort elsewhere too.

Gail seemed to guess what Perez was thinking. 'I was lucky with my husband. He was a good man, loyal to his family, but there are lots of bad ones out there.' She gave a sad little smile. 'I met a few of them when I was younger.'

'Tell me about your husband's accident.'

She didn't answer for a while. She'd finished mending the hen house now and started to gather up her tools into a canvas bag.

'It was the start of the autumn,' she said. 'There were fallen leaves everywhere and then it started to rain, so the roads were very slippery. Much worse than ice. John skidded on his way back to the farm after a night in the village. A witness says there was another car driving much too fast the other way, and that's why John had to swerve. But that driver was never found.'

'That must be hard. Especially if people in the village are saying he'd been drinking and it was his own fault.'

Gail shrugged again. 'I could let it eat away at me. All those "what ifs". What if the other driver had been more careful? What if John had stayed home that night? But it does no good. I have our daughter, Grace, to think about.'

Perez didn't answer. He'd had a sudden, strange thought. He was wondering if Anna Blackwell had a car and if she'd been out the night of John's accident. If Anna had caused Gail's husband's death, that might provide a motive for murder. Then Perez decided he was being crazy. He couldn't see Gail as a killer. And besides, she'd been at the farm the whole night of Anna's death, looking after two fatherless children.

He walked with Gail back towards the farm-house, carrying the piece of rotten wood she'd replaced.

'Will you find out what really happened?' she asked.

This time it was his turn to shrug. 'I don't know. I haven't got much time left. I have to go home to Shetland tomorrow.'

'Perhaps that's a good thing,' Gail said. 'Perhaps we should forget about Anna's death and remember her life. That's what I try to do with John. We should let the dead rest in peace.'

Perez didn't know what to say. He wanted to tell her that the love of his life had died not long before and so he understood how Gail was feeling. He had decided to let Fran rest in peace too. But in the end he just nodded and got into his car.

As Perez pulled out of the farm track onto the road, he saw a dark figure standing in a lay-by, staring. Perez was sure it was the man who'd been watching his hotel the night before. He slammed on the brakes and backed up the road to the lay-by, but the man had gone. It was as if he'd vanished into thin air. He must have run off into the trees. It made Perez wonder if his mind had been playing tricks and if the watcher had ever been there at all.

12

The Doctor

Back in Stonebridge, Perez decided that the time had come to talk to Tom King. Sarah had told him not to, but he couldn't see any way of reaching an end to the case without speaking to the doctor. It was lunchtime – in the school playground the children were racing and shouting – and this might be a good moment to find Tom free.

He went into the health centre and gave his name to the woman behind the desk.

'I'm sorry,' she said. 'Doctor King has just finished his surgery, so he's not seeing any more patients. Is it urgent?' The place was empty apart from the receptionist.

'I'm an old friend,' Perez said. 'Not a patient. Perhaps you could just tell Tom that I'm here.'

She looked at him over her glasses and then left through a door behind her. He could hear muttered voices, then Tom appeared.

'Jimmy,' he said. 'What are you doing in this neck of the woods? Does Sarah know you're in Stonebridge?'

Perez saw again how tired and tense the doctor looked. 'I'm here because Sarah asked me to come. She thought you could both use my help.'

'She didn't say she'd been in touch with you,' Tom said. He struggled to keep his voice pleasant, but Perez could sense the resentment.

'We need to talk,' Perez said quietly. 'I think you can guess what this is all about.'

There was a pause, and for a long moment Jimmy thought Tom would refuse, but then he nodded. 'Let's go for a walk,' he said at last. 'I can't think in here. I need some fresh air.'

Tom led Perez down a footpath next to the river and under the stone bridge that had given its name to the village. Soon they were out in open farmland. Bare fields stretched on either side of the water.

'It's about Anna Blackwell,' Perez said. 'How did you know her?'

Tom looked away and didn't answer. They walked on in silence.

'Were you lovers?' Perez asked. 'Are you the father of her child?'

'*No!*' Tom cried. He paused. 'Is that what Sarah thinks?'

'She's worried and upset. I'm not sure that she knows *what* to think.'

Tom stopped suddenly and looked out over the water. It was so cold that his breath came in clouds. 'I promised not to tell anyone. Not even Sarah.'

'I have to find out what's been going on,' Perez said. 'Anna didn't commit suicide. I'm sure of that now. She was murdered. This isn't a time for secrets.'

Tom turned sharply towards Perez. 'My secret has absolutely nothing to do with Anna's death.'

'I'm sorry. You'll have to trust me on this. You have to tell me what you know.'

There was a moment of silence while they stared at each other. At last Tom set off again along the path and started talking. He looked ahead of him, not at Perez.

'You're right. I do know the name of Lucy's father.'

'Who is it?'

There was another pause. 'My brother, Miles. He's always had a taste for younger women. Anna was at university with his daughter and the girls became friends. Miles met Anna at a party at his home in Edinburgh. They had a fling and she got pregnant. She refused to get rid of the child. Miles asked me to sort things out with her, make sure that she was OK and had somewhere to live.' Tom paused again. 'I think he did care for her in his own way.'

'But he was a high-profile MP?' Perez said. 'He didn't want the fact that he'd fathered a child with a young student to be made public?'

'Of course he didn't.' Tom sounded bitter. 'He has hopes of a government job after the election. His wife's a wealthy woman and he doesn't want to upset her. I had to promise to keep Anna's child secret.'

'But you tried to help her?'

'Of course! I went to see her in Edinburgh to check she had everything she needed. She wouldn't take money from Miles. Then she applied for a job at the school here, and I was happy to let her rent the house I own in the village.' Tom paused. 'She was a great young woman, full of life and energy. I thought Miles had treated her badly and that she could use some support. Perhaps you know that her parents have problems of their own.'

'You let Lucy be taken into care,' Perez said. 'She's your niece. How could you do that?'

Tom didn't answer and Perez changed tack.

'Sarah saw you together,' he said. 'It was in the health centre. You and Lucy looked so alike that Sarah assumed you were the girl's father.'

Tom frowned. 'So that's why she started the petition to get Anna sacked from the school.' He sounded shocked. 'I didn't realise. She tried to talk to me about Anna, but I could only think about my promise to my brother.' He stopped in his tracks again.

Looking back towards Stonebridge, Perez could see the small grey houses and the wood smoke rising from the chimneys in the still air. It looked very peaceful.

'What does this mean?' Tom said. He turned and started to pace back towards the village. 'Does it help you find out who killed Anna?'

Perez didn't know what to say to that. He had no idea how important these new facts were. He needed time to think about what he'd just learned.

'I'm not sure. But I do know that you have to talk to Sarah,' he said. 'It's making her ill thinking that you might have had a child with a younger woman. She'll keep your brother's secret. If you still think it's a secret worth keeping . . .'

'Of course you're right.' Tom was walking so quickly now that he was almost running. 'I've just been so stupid. I'll go home and see her this afternoon. I have a couple of hours free. We can talk while the children are in school.'

Perez followed him back to the surgery and stood in the car park until Tom had driven away. He had a sudden sense of being watched and shifted his gaze to the street. Again the strange man was standing at some distance, close to the entrance of the school, and staring at him. It was as if he was desperate to speak to Perez but couldn't quite find the nerve to approach him.

'Come here,' Perez shouted. 'I might be able to help you.' But the words just seemed to scare the man and he turned and ran away.

13

The Stranger

Perez chased the man who'd been following him. He was certain that this stranger held the answer to the mystery of Anna Blackwell's death. The man took a road that Perez hadn't explored yet. It led quickly out of the village and rose into dense woodland. Perez thought these must be the woods he'd seen at the back of Sarah and Tom's house. They were conifer trees, planted very close together, and they blocked out most of the light. It was as if night had come early.

The man left the road and took a path through the woods. Perez was fit, but the stranger seemed to run without effort. He knew just where he was going and Perez soon felt lost. He was out of his comfort zone. He was used to Shetland with its open hills and big skies. There were few trees in the islands and he'd never been in a forest as dense and dark as this before. All he could see was a glimpse of a shadow heading into the undergrowth. Then even that was gone and Perez knew that the man had escaped him.

Despite the cold, Perez was sweating after his run. He stood still for a moment and tried to figure out the way back to the road. The little light that was left was fading, and he knew he'd have no chance of finding his way back to the village in the dark. He stumbled through the trees, hoping to see lights from houses or cars.

And all the time his mind was working. He'd figured out who he'd been following. A glimpse of the stranger's face had shown a family likeness to a person Perez had come to know well. The man must be Sandy Kerr, Gail's brother. He'd been one of the people in the wedding photo at the farmhouse. This case was all about family secrets, Perez thought. That was why it had been so hard to find out what had been going on, to find out what had led to Anna's murder.

Perez lost his footing and slid down a steep bank, landing on a hard surface that scraped his hands. Tarmac. At last, and quite by chance, he'd found the road.

Jimmy started breathing more easily, and the panic he'd felt when he was surrounded by trees slowly left him. He just had to follow the road back to Stonebridge and his hotel. He knew that

Sandy Kerr lived with his sister. It shouldn't be hard to find him and see what he had to say. Perez had the feeling that Sandy wanted to explain what had happened to Anna. He was ready to talk.

Perez had walked a few hundred yards when he heard the sound of an engine behind him. He moved to the side of the road. He was tempted to flag down the car and get a lift into the village. Now that he had an idea what might have happened here in Stonebridge, Perez wanted the case finished as soon as possible. He longed to be on the ferry back to Shetland. He was missing his daughter, Cassie, and his house by the water. He could never be truly happy when he was away from the sea.

Perez put out his hand to wave at the car. In Shetland people were used to giving lifts, and in more remote places they always stopped for walkers. Surely it would be the same in a village like Stonebridge, a village that claimed to be friendly?

But the car showed no sign of stopping or even slowing down. Perez thought perhaps the driver hadn't seen him, and resigned himself to walking back to the hotel. After all, it couldn't be that far. He stood on the verge to allow the car to pass safely. The road was very narrow here.

Then he saw that instead of passing carefully by, the car was heading straight towards him.

All Perez could see was the glare of headlights as he jumped from the grass bank into the ditch that separated the road from the trees. There was a screech of brakes as the car careered away from him. It all happened so quickly and it was so dark that he couldn't even make out the type of car. There was no way he could see who the driver was.

Perez stood shaking by the side of the road. He felt angry, not just because the unknown driver had tried to kill him, but because he'd been foolish enough to put himself in danger.

He had Cassie to look after now, and he should be more careful. He'd bruised his leg jumping into the ditch. It was full of snow, his feet were soaking wet, and his hands were still bleeding from the fall onto the road. He thought his dis-comfort served him right and he started limping back to the village.

14

The Confession

At the hotel, Perez managed to get to his room without being seen by the nosy landlady, Elspeth. He would have struggled to explain the torn trousers and the muddy footprints left on the lobby floor. Jimmy jumped into the shower and changed into clean clothes and at last he stopped feeling cold. Then he phoned Robert Anderson, the local cop, with whom he'd worked in Aberdeen.

'Is there any chance you could get over to Stonebridge this evening?'

'You think you've solved the case for me, do you, Jimmy?' Anderson's voice made the question sound like a joke.

Perez answered seriously though. 'I think so.'

Now Anderson sounded surprised. 'You're telling me you've got enough evidence to make an arrest?'

'No physical evidence yet, but I'm sure there'll be fingerprints on the note I found in Anna's bedroom.' Perez paused. 'Besides, I think the culprit might be ready to confess.'

Then he remembered the car hurtling towards him in the dark forest and he wasn't so sure.

They arranged for Anderson to join him at the hotel. 'As soon as you can, Robbie,' Perez said. 'Our culprit is desperate now. We don't want them running away.'

Jimmy didn't bother looking out of his window when he was waiting for Anderson to arrive. He knew that the watcher would no longer be there.

They drove in Anderson's car to the Kerrs' farm. 'This is my patch, Jimmy,' Anderson had said when Perez had offered to drive. 'Besides, look at the state of you, man. You're in no fit state to be behind a wheel.'

In the farmyard, a blue VW was parked beside Gail's Land Rover. There were lights on in the house. Perez realised it must be time for the family's dinner. He wondered if they should have waited until they could be sure Grace would be in bed. He didn't want to talk to Gail and her brother in front of the little girl.

Gail opened the door to them. 'Inspector,' she said. She might have been surprised to see

82

them, but her voice was as cool as it always was. 'What can I do for you?'

'Is Sandy in?'

'Yes,' she said. 'He's not long got back from work.'

'And Grace?'

'Oh, she's in her onesie in the living room watching her favourite DVD. That's her pre-bedtime routine.' Gail smiled and stood aside to let them in.

Sandy was in the kitchen with the remains of a meal in front of him. It seemed he hadn't been very hungry. Perez saw straightaway that he was the strange watcher, the man he'd followed into the woods. Sandy shifted in his seat but gave no other sign that he knew the inspector.

'We have to talk,' Perez said.

Gail took her place at the table and Anderson joined them. Perez remained standing.

'What's going on?' Gail said. 'I don't understand.'

Perez ignored her and directed his question at Sandy. 'Were you in love with Anna Blackwell, Mr Kerr?'

'Don't be stupid, Inspector,' Gail said. 'Sandy's engaged to Emma Watt, who lives in the village. The wedding's planned for the spring.'

'Please answer, Mr Kerr.' Perez kept his voice quiet.

'I adored Anna,' Sandy said. 'I fell for her the moment I saw her.'

'How did you meet?'

'I often help out with Grace.' Sandy was leaning forward across the table. He was eager to explain now. 'My hours with the forestry aren't fixed. I picked her up from school one day. Anna had a message for Gail and we chatted for a while.'

'Were you helping out with Grace on the night that Anna Blackwell died?' Perez asked.

Sandy shifted in his seat and didn't answer.

'Did you look after Grace and Lucy for Gail on the night that Anna died?' This time the question was louder, more forceful. When there was still no reply, Perez went on. 'You'd have known Lucy, after all, if you'd been spending time with her mother. Both girls would have been happy to stay with you.'

When Sandy spoke it was almost in a whisper. 'Yes, I was babysitting that night. Gail said she needed to go out. There was something she needed to sort out, she said. Something urgent. I wanted to tell you.' His eyes were pleading.

'That's why you were waiting outside the hotel?'

Sandy nodded. 'But then I thought Gail had been so good to me, and she'd just lost her husband. I couldn't bring myself to do it. How could I accuse her of murder when she's been through so much?'

Gail started to whimper. The noise wasn't loud enough to disturb the child in the next room, but it was piercing. It seemed to cut through Perez's skin to his bone.

He turned to the woman. 'You set up a meeting with Anna Blackwell and you killed her. And this afternoon you tried to kill me. You were worried your brother would pluck up the courage to tell me what was going on, and you drove straight at me in your Land Rover. You must have had Grace with you. How could you do that?'

Gail didn't answer. She was sitting with her head in her hands and tears ran down her cheeks.

15

The Conclusion

Inspectors Anderson and Perez sat in the lounge bar of the Stonebridge Hotel. It was late and there were no other drinkers. It occurred to Perez that if the bar was always this empty, the owners were making very little money from the place. But perhaps it was busier in the summer. Then there would be tourists in the village and the bar would be full of talk and laughter.

'I don't understand why the Kerr woman killed Anna Blackwell.' Anderson was staring into his beer. 'You can't blame us for missing that one, Jimmy.'

'She was worried about losing the farm,' Perez said. 'Sandy's wage was all that was keeping the place going. Gail knew that Anna was full of life and ideas. She must have known that the teacher would want to move on after a while. Gail and Grace wouldn't have been able to stay at the farm without Sandy's wage to support them.'

'It doesn't seem much of a motive.' Anderson looked up from his glass. 'And wasn't Sandy going to move out anyway? I thought he was engaged.'

'But to a local girl,' Perez said. 'Someone Gail knew and liked. Someone who'd probably be happy to move into the farm in the end, and who'd be able to help Gail carry out all the plans John had for the place. Anna was the sort of girl who would have had plans of her own.'

'All the same . . .'Anderson wasn't convinced.

'You have to realise that Gail couldn't see things clearly. She'd married later than most people and thought she'd found her soulmate. She and John and Grace were the family she'd dreamed of. Then John died.'

To Perez this sounded so like the story of him and his wife Fran and their Cassie that he struggled to keep control. He worried that he might break down. As Gail had done when Anderson arrested her.

'After realising it must have been Gail who drove towards me in the Land Rover today,' Perez went on, 'I wondered if she'd killed her husband in the same way. If he'd had an affair and Gail had killed him out of revenge. But I believe that was just a tragic accident. She loved the bones of him.'

I thought Gail was being so strong, he thought, and all the time grief was eating her away inside. The idea that Sandy might leave her too and she might have to sell the farm that held so many happy memories was enough to tip her over the edge.

'Talk me through it, Jimmy,' Anderson said. 'Tell me what really happened to Anna Blackwell.'

'The whole thing was planned in advance,' Perez said. 'Gail asked Lucy to the farm for a sleepover and suggested that the two women might meet up on the same night. Gail said that Sandy could babysit so she'd be happy to go to Anna's house. The note that I found was Anna's reply. She probably sent it home in Grace's schoolbag.'

'How did Gail know that Sandy and Anna were having a fling?' Anderson took a long drink of beer.

'Sandy told her that he planned to break off his engagement. He explained that he'd fallen for Anna.' Perez paused and went on to describe how Anna had been killed. 'On the night of the 10th, Gail left the girls with Sandy and drove into Stonebridge. I think she parked round the corner from the teacher's house because Anna's neighbour didn't see or hear a car.'

Perez imagined the scene. Anna had prepared the house. She might not have felt well enough for a full spring clean, but she'd bought flowers to cheer the place up, and she'd put wine in the fridge to chill. She'd have pictured a friendly chat with the woman who might one day become her sister-in-law.

'Gail would only have had one glass of wine,' he said. 'She'd have explained that she couldn't drink because she was driving. At one point she went upstairs and crushed the pills she found in Anna's bedroom into a powder. Everyone in the village knew Anna was taking antidepressants.

'That was when Gail made her big mistake. The note from Anna was in her pocket and it dropped out on the dressing table. Without the note we would never have been able to prove what had happened.'

Jimmy Perez paused for breath and looked at Anderson, who was listening intently.

'Gail went back downstairs,' he continued. 'Anna would have been quite tipsy at that point. She wasn't used to drinking. It wouldn't have been hard for Gail to tip the crushed pills into her wine without Anna noticing. They must have dissolved very quickly. She waited until Anna fell into a deep sleep, then she went into the kitchen, washed out her own glass and put it away. I'm sure you'll find traces of the drug in the unwashed glass.'

'Then she drove home,' Anderson said, 'as if nothing had happened.'

Perez nodded. 'The next morning she took Lucy back and seemed as shocked as everyone else that Anna was dead.'

The inspector sipped his beer. 'Freda, one of the other teachers, had already started the rumours about Anna and Tom. Freda hated the fact that she'd been replaced by a younger woman. Gail spread the gossip so that if you did decide that Anna had been murdered, no one would suspect that she was involved in the killing.'

'But her brother did suspect,' Anderson said.

'He was the only person who knew how badly Gail had been affected by her husband's death. And he knew how passionate she was about the farm. Sandy heard that I was asking questions and he came to the hotel to talk to me. But he couldn't quite do it. He couldn't quite bring himself to accuse his sister of murder.'

Anderson emptied his glass. 'I suppose I should

thank you for clearing the case up for me, Jimmy.'

'I'm sorry if you felt I was treading on your toes.'

'Aye well.' Anderson grinned. 'Just don't think of coming to meddle on my patch again. Or I might come up to Shetland to work on one of your cases.'

'You'd be very welcome, Robbie. Any time.' Perez smiled back.

'Are you joking? Ferries and small planes make me feel sick before I step onto them. You're quite safe, Jimmy. I'll leave you on your islands in peace.'

16

The Letter

Jimmy Perez left the next morning without saying goodbye to Tom and Sarah King. In a place like Stonebridge, news of Gail's arrest would soon get out and the gossips would have another target for their chatter. Tom and Sarah would be left in peace.

It was a calm sailing on the ferry, and Perez's friends brought his daughter, Cassie, to meet the boat when it got into Lerwick after the overnight crossing. He dropped his stepdaughter at school and went into work. Over the next few weeks he was busy with everyday police work in Shetland and he'd almost forgotten the case in Stonebridge when a letter arrived from Sarah.

The envelope contained a photo, and it was this that slipped onto the table first. The picture had been taken in the Kings' garden. It showed Tom and Sarah and the children wrapped up against the cold on a bright, clear day. There were Christmas lights on the fir trees on each side of the front door.

When Perez looked again he saw that there were three children in the photo, not two. The third child was smaller and she had dark curls and a wide, beaming smile. It was Lucy, Anna's daughter.

Perez read the letter that went with the photo. It had been written by Sarah.

Thanks so much for all your help. You can't know what a difference you made to our lives. We've had a fab Christmas and that was all down to you. I wanted to tell you that we've become Lucy's guardians and we hope to adopt her. You know I always hoped for a big family and her cousins love her to bits. Now my life's perfect.

Perez smiled to himself and stuck the photo onto the fridge.

About Quick Reads

Quick Reads are brilliant short new books written by bestselling writers. They are perfect for regular readers wanting a fast and satisfying read, but they are also ideal for adults who are discovering reading for pleasure for the first time.

Since Quick Reads was founded in 2006, over 4.5 million copies of more than a hundred titles have been sold or distributed. Quick Reads are available in paperback, in ebook and from your local library.

To find out more about Quick Reads titles, visit

www.readingagency.org.uk/quickreads

Tweet us 🐦 @Quick_Reads #GalaxyQuickReads

Quick Reads is part of The Reading Agency,
a national charity that inspires more people to read more, encourages them to share their enjoyment of reading with others and celebrates the difference that reading makes to all our lives.
www.readingagency.org.uk Tweet us @readingagency

The Reading Agency Ltd • Registered number: 3904882 (England & Wales) Registered charity number: 1085443 (England & Wales) Registered Office: Free Word Centre, 60 Farringdon Road, London, EC1R 3GA The Reading Agency is supported using public funding by Arts Council England.

We would like to thank all our funders:

LOTTERY FUNDED

Start a new chapter

A Baby at the Beach Café

Lucy Diamond

Evie loves running her beach café in Cornwall but with a baby on the way, she's been told to put her feet up. Let someone else take over? Not likely.

Helen's come to Cornwall to escape the stress of city living. She hopes a seaside life will be the answer to all her dreams. When she sees a job advertised at the café it sounds perfect.

But the two women clash and sparks fly . . . and then events take a dramatic turn. Can the pair of them put aside their differences in a crisis?

Available in paperback, ebook and from your local library

Pan Books

Why not start a reading group?

If you have enjoyed this book, why not share your next Quick Read with friends, colleagues, or neighbours?

The Reading Agency also runs **Reading Groups for Everyone** which helps you discover and share new books. Find a reading group near you, or register a group you already belong to and get free books and offers from publishers at **readinggroups.org**

A reading group is a great way to get the most out of a book and is easy to arrange. All you need is a group of people, a place to meet and a date and time that works for everyone.

Use the first meeting to decide which book to read first and how the group will operate. Conversation doesn't have to stick rigidly to the book. Here are some suggested themes for discussions:

- How important was the plot?
- What messages are in the book?
- Discuss the characters – were they believable and could you relate to them?
- How important was the setting to the story?
- Are the themes timeless?
- Personal reactions – what did you like or not like about the book?

There is a free toolkit with lots of ideas to help you run a Quick Reads reading group at **www.readingagency.org.uk/quickreads**

Share your experiences of your group on Twitter @Quick_Reads #GalaxyQuickReads

Continuing your reading journey

As well as Quick Reads, The Reading Agency runs lots of programmes to help keep you reading.

Reading Ahead invites you to pick six reads and record your reading in a diary in order to get a certificate. If you're thinking about improving your reading or would like to read more, then this is for you. Find out more at **www.readingahead.org.uk**

World Book Night is an annual celebration of reading and books on 23 April, which sees passionate volunteers give out books in their communities to share their love of reading. Find out more at **worldbooknight.org**

Reading together with a child will help them to develop a lifelong love of reading. Our **Chatterbooks** children's reading groups and **Summer Reading Challenge** inspire children to read more and share the books they love. Find out more at **readingagency.org.uk/children**

Find more books for new readers at

- **www.readingahead.org.uk/find-a-read**
- **www.newisland.ie**
- **www.barringtonstoke.co.uk**